Children's Books:

Easter is Cancelled!

Sally Huss

Easter is Cancelled!

ISBN: 0692636226
ISBN 13: 9780692636220

It was Eastertime and everyone was getting ready,

everyone that is except the Easter Bunny.

This was odd, yes, and not one bit funny.

It was particularly not funny for the chickens

who were laying the eggs…

And not funny too for the kittens who were dyeing them,
straining their hind legs.

It was not funny at all for the dogs who were making

the chocolate candy…

Or the ducks who were wrapping the candy

to make it look dandy.

And it wasn't so funny for pig after pig

Who were gathering grass for the baskets,

dig after dig.

And it was especially not funny for the geese and the swans

Who were struggling to make Easter baskets

out of dried palm fronds.

But what was the Easter Bunny doing

while the other animals were working so hard?

He was making a sign on a big, yellow card.

He was cancelling Easter, their favorite occasion.

"Oh my, oh my," they cried, "this is a dreadful situation."

What could be the reason for him not taking part?

He flopped down on his hammock and announced,

"I've simply lost heart!

No one ever thanks me for the work I do,

Organizing Easter and overseeing all of you.

The kids take me for granted each and every year,

Not one word of thanks," he said. Down his cheek rolled a tear.

Hmmm. This was serious, all the animals agreed.

"We need some help here. Yes, that's what we need."

Just at that moment, high above them,

among the leaves on a branch

Sat a wise and thoughtful owl

watching over them with a one-eyed glance.

"Whoo, whoo," he hooted, "who could you ask

who sees things more clearly…

Than myself, who can solve your problem quite easily?"

"Right you are," answered the animals on the ground.

They waited as the owl spun his head around.

"To clarify," he continued, "the problem is that the big bunny

in charge of this celebration

Has decided to sit down on the job,

abandoning his obligation."

"That's right," they said. "That's it. He just quit!

What can be done?

The Easter Bunny feels his efforts

are appreciated by none."

The owl thought for a moment,

then spoke with such knowing,

"Find a child with a smile, one who is just glowing.

Get him to explain to the bunny the importance of Easter

to children all over the world.

Tell him how much they love and appreciate him,

every boy and every girl.

Let him know they draw pictures of him

and read books about him.

They cherish him dearly and can't do without him.

Make him feel important. Make him feel proud.

That should bring him out of his gloomy, gray cloud."

Just then, skipping down the path nearby

Was the perfect, bright-faced little guy.

He was happy and full of good cheer.

Certainly he would be the one to make it clear.

After telling the boy what they needed…

The boy spoke to the Easter Bunny and obviously succeeded…

Because the Easter Bunny jumped up, put on his apron,

And went back to work without hesitation.

"Easter is on again," he said. "Hand me that brush."

He went back to painting eggs with a tremendous, great rush.

But what had the boy told the bunny, the animals wanted to know.

"I told him the only thing he needed to know…

That the most important things are the things we can't see,

Things like love and trust, and responsibility.

He must trust that what he does is valued and good

And be responsible by doing the things that he should.

That's when he decided that being the Easter Bunny

was well worth his while

And got back on the job with his usual smile."

The animals applauded the boy's efforts and turned to their boss

Who said, "Yes, making a happy day for others is never a loss.

I do what I love and I love what I do,

Especially now that I know that others love it too.

From now on, there will always be an Easter Day.

It warms my heart, I really must say!"

The end,
but not the end
of appreciating
the efforts of others.

At the end of this book you will find a Certificate of Merit that may be issued to any child who has fulfilled the requirements stated in the Certificate. This fine Certificate will easily fit into a 5"x7" frame, and happily suit any girl or boy who receives it!

Sally writes new books all the time. If you would like to be alerted when one of her new books becomes available or when one of her books is offered FREE on Amazon, sign up here: http://www.sallyhuss.com/kids-books.html.

If you liked *Easter is Cancelled*, please be kind enough to post a short review on Amazon. Here is the link: http://amzn.com/B01BCUA3IU.

Here are a few Sally Huss books you might enjoy. They may be found on Amazon as e-books or in soft cover.

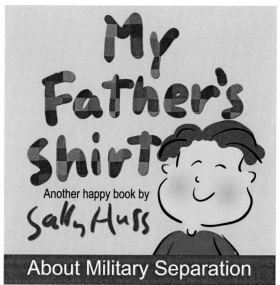

http://amzn.com/B018JQP8S0

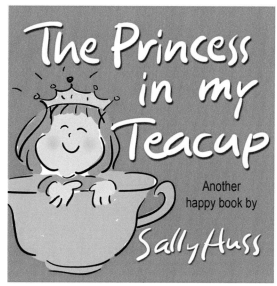

http://amzn.com/B00NG4EDH8

http://amzn.com/B0125714B4

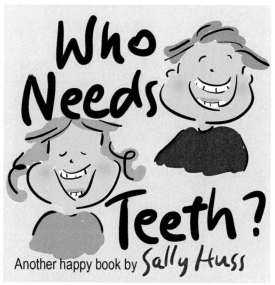

http://amzn.com/B00MT5TERO

About the Author/Illustrator

Sally Huss

"Bright and happy," "light and whimsical" have been the catch phrases attached to the writings and art of Sally Huss for over 30 years. Sweet images dance across all of Sally's creations, whether in the form of children's books, paintings, wallpaper, ceramics, baby bibs, purses, clothing, or her King Features syndicated newspaper panel "Happy Musings."

Sally creates children's books to uplift the lives of children and hopes you will join her in this effort by helping spread her happy messages.

Sally is a graduate of USC with a degree in Fine Art and through the years has had 26 of her own licensed art galleries throughout the world.

This certificate may be cut out, framed, and presented to any child who has earned it.

Certificate of Merit

_____
(Name)

The child named above is awarded this Certificate of Merit for:

*Working well with others
*Being responsible
*Appreciating the efforts of others

Presented by: _____ Date: _____

Made in the USA
San Bernardino, CA
22 March 2016